The Shawl

The Shawl

A Story and Novella

Cynthia Ozick

JONATHAN CAPE
LONDON

First published in Great Britain 1991
Jonathan Cape, 20 Vauxhall Bridge Road, London sw1v 2sa
© Cynthia Ozick 1980, 1983

Cynthia Ozick has asserted her right under the Copyright, Designs
and Patents Act, 1988, to be identified as the author of this work

The two stories comprising this work, 'The Shawl' and 'Rosa',
were originally published in *The New Yorker*

A CIP catalogue record for this book is available from the
British Library

isbn 0-224-03081-7

Printed in Great Britain by
St Edmundsbury Press, Bury St Edmunds, Suffolk

dein goldenes Haar Margarete
dein aschenes Haar Sulamith

PAUL CELAN, 'Todesfuge'

Contents

The Shawl

Stella, cold, cold, the coldness of hell. How they walked on the roads together, Rosa with Magda curled up between sore breasts, Magda wound up in the shawl. Sometimes Stella carried Magda. But she was jealous of Magda. A thin girl of fourteen, too small, with thin breasts of her own, Stella wanted to be wrapped in a shawl, hidden away, asleep, rocked by the march, a baby, a round infant in arms. Magda took Rosa's nipple, and Rosa never stopped walking, a walking cradle. There was not enough milk; sometimes Magda sucked air; then she screamed. Stella was ravenous. Her knees were tumors on sticks, her elbows chicken bones.

Rosa did not feel hunger; she felt light, not like

someone walking but like someone in a faint, in trance, arrested in a fit, someone who is already a floating angel, alert and seeing everything, but in the air, not there, not touching the road. As if teetering on the tips of her fingernails. She looked into Magda's face through a gap in the shawl: a squirrel in a nest, safe, no one could reach her inside the little house of the shawl's windings. The face, very round, a pocket mirror of a face: but it was not Rosa's bleak complexion, dark like cholera, it was another kind of face altogether, eyes blue as air, smooth feathers of hair nearly as yellow as the Star sewn into Rosa's coat. You could think she was one of *their* babies.

Rosa, floating, dreamed of giving Magda away in one of the villages. She could leave the line for a minute and push Magda into the hands of any woman on the side of the road. But if she moved out of line they might shoot. And even if she fled the line for half a second and pushed the shawl-bundle at a stranger, would the woman take it? She might be surprised, or afraid; she might drop the shawl, and Magda would fall out and strike her head and die. The little round head. Such a good child, she gave up screaming, and sucked now only for the taste of the drying nipple itself. The neat grip of the tiny gums. One mite of a tooth tip sticking up in the bottom gum, how shining, an elfin tomb-stone of white marble gleaming there. Without com-plaining, Magda relinquished Rosa's teats, first the left, then the right; both were cracked, not a sniff of milk. The duct-crevice extinct, a dead volcano, blind eye, chill hole, so Magda took the corner of the shawl and milked it instead. She sucked and sucked, flooding the threads with wetness. The shawl's good flavor, milk of linen.

It was a magic shawl, it could nourish an infant for three days and three nights. Magda did not die, she stayed alive, although very quiet. A peculiar smell, of cinnamon and almonds, lifted out of her mouth. She held her eyes open every moment, forgetting how to blink or nap, and Rosa and sometimes Stella studied their blueness. On the road they raised one burden of a leg after another and studied Magda's face. 'Aryan,' Stella said, in a voice grown as thin as a string; and Rosa thought how Stella gazed at Magda like a young canni-bal. And the time that Stella said 'Aryan,' it sounded to Rosa as if Stella had really said 'Let us devour her.'

But Magda lived to walk. She lived that long, but she did not walk very well, partly because she was only fifteen months old, and partly because the spindles of her legs could not hold up her fat belly. It was fat with air, full and round. Rosa gave almost all her food to Magda, Stella gave nothing; Stella was ravenous, a growing child herself, but not growing much. Stella did not menstruate. Rosa did not menstruate. Rosa was ravenous, but also not; she learned from Magda how to drink the taste of a finger in one's mouth. They were in a place without pity, all pity was annihilated in Rosa, she looked at Stella's bones without pity. She was sure that Stella was waiting for Magda to die so she could put her teeth into the little thighs.

Rosa knew Magda was going to die very soon; she should have been dead already, but she had been buried away deep inside the magic shawl, mistaken there for the shivering mound of Rosa's breasts; Rosa clung to the shawl as if it covered only herself. No one took it away from her. Magda was mute. She never cried. Rosa hid her in the barracks, under the shawl, but she knew that one day someone would inform; or one day someone, not even Stella, would steal Magda to eat her. When Magda began to walk Rosa knew that Magda was going to die very soon, something would happen. She was afraid to fall asleep; she slept with the weight of her thigh on Magda's body; she was afraid she would smother Magda under her thigh. The weight of Rosa was becoming less and less; Rosa and Stella were slowly turning into air.

Magda was quiet, but her eyes were horribly alive, like blue tigers. She watched. Sometimes she laughed – it seemed a laugh, but how could it be? Magda had never seen anyone laugh. Still, Magda laughed at her shawl when the wind blew its corners, the bad wind with pieces of black in it, that made Stella's and Rosa's eyes tear. Magda's eyes were always clear and tearless. She watched like a tiger. She guarded her shawl. No one could touch it; only Rosa could touch it. Stella was not allowed. The shawl was Magda's own baby, her pet, her little sister. She tangled herself up in it and sucked on one of the corners when she wanted to be very still.

Then Stella took the shawl away and made Magda die.

Afterward Stella said: 'I was cold.'

And afterward she was always cold, always. The cold went into her heart: Rosa saw that Stella's heart was cold. Magda flopped onward with her little pencil legs scribbling this way and that, in search of the shawl; the pencils faltered at the barracks opening, where the light began. Rosa saw and pursued. But already Magda was in the square outside the barracks, in the jolly light. It was the roll-call arena. Every morning Rosa had to conceal Magda under the shawl against a wall of the barracks and go out and stand in the arena with Stella and hundreds of others, sometimes for hours, and Magda, deserted, was quiet under the shawl, sucking on her corner. Every day Magda was silent, and so she did not die. Rosa saw that today Magda was going to die, and at the same time a fearful joy ran in Rosa's two palms, her fingers were on fire, she was astonished, febrile: Magda, in the sunlight, swaying on her pencil legs, was howling. Ever since the drying up of Rosa's nipples, ever since Magda's last scream on the road, Magda had been devoid of any syllable; Magda was a mute. Rosa believed that something had gone wrong with her vocal cords, with her windpipe, with the cave of her larynx; Magda was defective, without a voice; perhaps she was deaf; there might be something amiss with her intelligence; Magda was dumb. Even the laugh that came when the ash-stippled wind made a clown out of Magda's shawl was only the air-blown showing of her teeth. Even when the lice, head lice and body lice, crazed her so that she became as wild as one of the big rats that plundered the barracks at daybreak looking for carrion, she rubbed and scratched and kicked and bit and rolled without a whimper. But now Magda's mouth was spilling a long viscous rope of clamor.

'Maaaa – '

It was the first noise Magda had ever sent out from her throat since the drying up of Rosa's nipples.

'Maaaa . . . aaa!'

Again! Magda was wavering in the perilous sunlight of the arena, scribbling on such pitiful little bent shins. Rosa saw. She saw that Magda was grieving for the loss of her shawl, she saw that Magda was going to die. A tide of commands hammered in Rosa's nipples: Fetch, get, bring! But she did not know which to go after first, Magda or the shawl. If she jumped out into the arena to snatch Magda up, the howling would not stop, because Magda would still not have the shawl; but if she ran back into the barracks to find the shawl, and if she found it, and if she came after Magda holding it and shaking it, then she would get Magda back, Magda would put the shawl in her mouth and turn dumb again.

Rosa entered the dark. It was easy to discover the

shawl. Stella was heaped under it, asleep in her thin bones. Rosa tore the shawl free and flew – she could fly, she was only air – into the arena. The sunheat murmured of another life, of butterflies in summer. The light was placid, mellow. On the other side of the steel fence, far away, there were green meadows speckled with dandelions and deep-colored violets; beyond them, even farther, innocent tiger lilies, tall, lifting their orange bonnets. In the barracks they spoke of 'flowers', of 'rain': excrement, thick turd-braids, and the slow stinking maroon waterfall that slunk down from the upper bunks, the stink mixed with a bitter fatty floating smoke that greased Rosa's skin. She stood for an instant at the margin of the arena. Sometimes the electricity inside the fence would seem to hum; even Stella said it was only an imagining, but Rosa heard real sounds in the wire: grainy sad voices. The farther she was from the fence, the more clearly the voices crowded at her. The lamenting voices strummed so convincingly, so passionately, it was impossible to suspect them of being phantoms. The voices told her to hold up the shawl, high; the voices told her to shake it, to whip with it, to unfurl it like a flag. Rosa lifted, shook, whipped, unfurled. Far off, very far, Magda leaned across her air-fed belly, reaching out with the rods of her arms. She was high up, elevated, riding someone's shoulder. But the shoulder that carried Magda was not coming toward Rosa and the shawl, it was drifting away, the speck of Magda was moving more and more into the smoky distance. Above the shoulder a helmet glinted. The light tapped the helmet and sparkled it into a goblet. Below the helmet a black body like a domino and a pair of black boots hurled themselves in the direction of the electrified fence. The electric voices began to chatter wildly. 'Maamaa, maaamaaa,' they all hummed together. How far Magda was from Rosa now, across the whole square, past a dozen barracks, all the way on the other side! She was no bigger than a moth.

All at once Magda was swimming through the air. The whole of Magda traveled through loftiness. She looked like a butterfly touching a silver vine. And the moment Magda's feathered round head and her pencil legs and balloonish belly and zigzag arms splashed against the fence, the steel voices went mad in their growling, urging Rosa to run and run to the spot where Magda had fallen from her flight against the electrified fence; but of course Rosa did not obey them. She only stood, because if she ran they would shoot, and if she tried to pick up the sticks of Magda's body they would shoot, and if she let the wolf's screech ascending now through the ladder of her skeleton break out, they would shoot; so she took Magda's shawl and filled her own mouth with it, stuffed it in and stuffed it in, until she was swallowing up the wolf's screech and tasting the cinnamon and almond depth of Magda's saliva; and Rosa drank Magda's shawl until it dried.

Rosa

Rosa Lublin, a madwoman and a scavenger, gave up
her store – she smashed it up herself – and moved to
Miami. It was a mad thing to do. In Florida she
became a dependent. Her niece in New York sent her
money and she lived among the elderly, in a dark hole,
a single room in a 'hotel'. There was an ancient
dresser-top refrigerator and a one-burner stove. Over
in a corner a round oak table brooded on its heavy
pedestal, but it was only for drinking tea. Her meals
she had elsewhere, in bed or standing at the sink –
sometimes toast with a bit of sour cream and half a
sardine, or a small can of peas heated in a Pyrex mug.
Instead of maid service there was a dumbwaiter on a
shrieking pulley. On Tuesdays and Fridays it swallowed

her meager bags of garbage. Squads of dying flies blackened the rope. The sheets on her bed were just as black – it was a five-block walk to the laundromat. The streets were a furnace, the sun an executioner. Every day without fail it blazed and blazed, so she stayed in her room and ate two bites of a hard-boiled egg in bed, with a writing board on her knees; she had lately taken to composing letters.

She wrote sometimes in Polish and sometimes in English, but her niece had forgotten Polish; most of the time Rosa wrote to Stella in English. Her English was crude. To her daughter Magda she wrote in the most excellent literary Polish. She wrote on the brittle sheets of abandoned stationery that inexplicably turned up in the cubbyholes of a blistered old desk in the lobby. Or she would ask the Cuban girl in the receptionist's cage for a piece of blank billing paper. Now and then she would find a clean envelope in the lobby bin; she would meticulously rip its seams and lay it out flat: it made a fine white square, the fresh face of a new letter.

The room was littered with these letters. It was hard to get them mailed – the post office was a block farther off than the laundromat, and the hotel lobby's stamp machine had been marked 'Out of Order' for years. There was an oval tin of sardines left open on the sink counter since yesterday. Already it smelled vomitous. She felt she was in hell. 'Golden and beautiful Stella,' she wrote to her niece. 'Where I put myself is in hell.

Once I thought the worst was the worst, after that nothing could be the worst. But now I see, even after the worst there's still more.' Or she wrote: 'Stella, my angel, my dear one, a devil climbs into you and ties up your soul and you don't even know it.'

To Magda she wrote: 'You have grown into a lioness. You are tawny and you stretch apart your furry toes in all their power. Whoever steals you steals her own death.'

Stella had eyes like a small girl's, like a doll's. Round, not big but pretty, bright skin underneath, fine pure skin above, tender eyebrows like rainbows and lashes as rich as embroidery. She had the face of a little bride. You could not believe from all this beauty, these doll's eyes, these buttercup lips, these baby's cheeks, you could not believe in what harmless containers the bloodsucker comes.

Sometimes Rosa had cannibal dreams about Stella: she was boiling her tongue, her ears, her right hand, such a fat hand with plump fingers, each nail tended and rosy, and so many rings, not modern rings but old-fashioned junkshop rings. Stella liked everything from Rosa's junkshop, everything used, old, lacy with other people's history. To pacify Stella, Rosa called her Dear One, Lovely, Beautiful; she called her Angel; she called her all these things for the sake of peace, but in reality Stella was cold. She had no heart. Stella, already nearly fifty years old, the Angel of Death.

The bed was black, as black as Stella's will. After a

while Rosa had no choice, she took a bundle of laundry in a shopping cart and walked to the laundromat. Though it was only ten in the morning, the sun was killing. Florida, why Florida? Because here they were shells like herself, already fried from the sun. All the same she had nothing in common with them. Old ghosts, old socialists: idealists. The Human Race was all they cared for. Retired workers, they went to lectures, they frequented the damp and shadowy little branch library. She saw them walking with Tolstoy under their arms, with Dostoyevsky. They knew good material. Whatever you wore they would feel between their fingers and give a name to: faille, corduroy, herringbone, shantung, jersey, worsted, velour, crepe. She heard them speak of bias, grosgrain, the 'season', the 'length'. Yellow they called mustard. What was pink to everyone else, to them was sunset; orange was tangerine; red, hot tomato. They were from the Bronx, from Brooklyn, lost neighborhoods, burned out. A few were from West End Avenue. Once she met an ex-vegetable-store owner from Columbus Avenue; his store was on Columbus Avenue, his residence not far, on West Seventieth Street, off Central Park. Even in the perpetual garden of Florida, he reminisced about his flowery green heads of romaine lettuce, his glowing strawberries, his sleek avocados.

It seemed to Rosa Lublin that the whole peninsula of Florida was weighted down with regret. Everyone had left behind a real life. Here they had nothing. They were all scarecrows, blown about under the murdering sunball with empty rib cages.

In the laundromat she sat on a cracked wooden bench and watched the round porthole of the washing machine. Inside, the surf of detergent bubbles frothed and slapped her underwear against the pane.

An old man sat cross-legged beside her, fingering a newspaper. She looked over and saw that the head-lines were all in Yiddish. In Florida the men were of higher quality than the women. They knew a little more of the world, they read newspapers, they lived for international affairs. Everything that happened in the Israeli Knesset they followed. But the women only recited meals they used to cook in their old lives – kugel, pirogen, latkes, blintzes, herring salad. Mainly the women thought about their hair. They went to hairdressers and came out into the brilliant day with plantlike crowns the color of zinnias. Sea-green paint on the eyelids. One could pity them: they were in love with rumors of their grandchildren, Katie at Bryn Mawr, Jeff at Princeton. To the grandchildren Florida was a slum, to Rosa it was a zoo.

She had no one but her cold niece in Queens, New York.

'Imagine this,' the old man next to her said. 'Just look, first he has Hitler, then he has Siberia, he's in a camp in Siberia! Next thing he gets away to Sweden, then he comes to New York and he peddles. He's a peddler, by now he's got a wife, he's got kids, so he opens a little store – just a little store, his wife is a sick woman, it's what you call a bargain store – '

'What?' Rosa said.

'A bargain store on Main Street, a place in Westchester, not even the Bronx. And they come in early in the morning, he didn't even hang out his shopping bags yet, robbers, muggers, and they choke him, they finish him off. From Siberia he lives for this day!'

Rosa said nothing.

'An innocent man alone in his store. Be glad you're not up there anymore. On the other hand, here it's no paradise neither. Believe me, when it comes to muggers and stranglers, there's no utopia nowhere.'

'My machine's finished,' Rosa said. 'I have to put in the dryer.' She knew about newspapers and their evil reports: a newspaper item herself. WOMAN AXES OWN BIZ. Rosa Lublin, 59, owner of a secondhand furniture store on Utica Avenue, Brooklyn, yesterday afternoon deliberately demolished . . . The *News* and the *Post*. A big photograph, Stella standing near with her mouth stretched and her arms wild. In the *Times*, six lines.

'Excuse me, I notice you speak with an accent.'

Rosa flushed. 'I was born somewhere else, not here.'

'I also was born somewhere else. You're a refugee? Berlin?'

'Warsaw.'

'I'm also from Warsaw! 1920 I left. 1906 I was born.'

'Happy birthday,' Rosa said. She began to pull her things out of the washing machine. They were twisted into each other like mixed-up snakes.

'Allow me,' said the old man. He put down his paper and helped her untangle. 'Imagine this,' he said. 'Two people from Warsaw meet in Miami, Florida. In 1910 I didn't dream of Miami, Florida.'

'My Warsaw isn't your Warsaw,' Rosa said.

'As long as your Miami, Florida, is my Miami, Florida.' Two whole long rows of glinting dentures smiled at her; he was proud to be a flirt. Together they shoved the snarled load into the dryer. Rosa put in two quarters, and the thundering hum began. They heard the big snaps on the belt of her dress with the blue stripes, the one that was torn in the armpit, under the left sleeve, clanging against the caldron's metal sides.

'You read Yiddish?' the old man said.

'No.'

'You can speak a few words maybe?'

'No.' My Warsaw isn't your Warsaw. But she remembered her grandmother's cradle-croonings: her grandmother was from Minsk. *Unter Reyzls vigele shteyt a klorvays tsigele.* How Rosa's mother despised those sounds! When the drying cycle ended, Rosa noticed that the old man handled the clothes like an expert. She was ashamed for him to touch her underpants. *Under Rosa's cradle there's a clear-white little*

25

goat . . . But he knew how to find a sleeve, wherever it might be hiding.

'What is it,' he asked, 'you're bashful?'

'No.'

'In Miami, Florida, people are more friendly. What,' he said, 'you're still afraid? Nazis we ain't got, even Ku Kluxers we ain't got. What kind of person are you, you're still afraid?'

'The kind of person,' Rosa said, 'is what you see. Thirty-nine years ago I was somebody else.'

'Thirty-nine years ago I wasn't so bad myself. I lost my teeth without a single cavity,' he bragged. 'Everything perfect. Periodontal disease.'

'*I* was a chemist almost. A physicist,' Rosa said. 'You think I wouldn't have been a scientist?' The thieves who took her life! All at once the landscape behind her eyes fell out of control: a bright field flashed; then a certain shadowy corridor leading to the laboratory supplies closet. The closet opened in her dreams also. Always she was hurtling down a veiled passage toward the closet. Retorts and microscopes were ranged on the shelves. Once, walking there, she was conscious of the coursing of her own ecstasy – her new brown shoes, laced and sober, her white coat, her hair cut short in bangs: a serious person of seventeen, ambitious, responsible, a future Marie Curie! One of her teachers in the high school praised her for what he said was a 'literary style' – oh, lost and kidnapped Polish! – and now she wrote and spoke English as

helplessly as this old immigrant. From Warsaw! Born
1906! She imagined what bitter ancient alley, dense
with stalls, cheap clothes strung on outdoor racks,
signs in jargoned Yiddish. Anyhow they called her
refugee. The Americans couldn't tell her apart from
this fellow with his false teeth and his dewlaps and his
rakehell reddish toupee bought God knows when or
where – Delancey Street, the Lower East Side. A
dandy. Warsaw! What did he know? In school she had
read Tuwim: such delicacy, such loftiness, such *Polish-
ness*. The Warsaw of her girlhood: a great light: she
switched it on, she wanted to live inside her eyes. The
curve of the legs of her mother's bureau. The strict
leather smell of her father's desk. The white tile tract
of the kitchen floor, the big pots breathing, a narrow
tower stair next to the attic . . . the house of her
girlhood laden with a thousand books. Polish, German,
French; her father's Latin books; the shelf of shy
literary periodicals her mother's poetry now and then
wandered through, in short lines like heated telegrams.
Cultivation, old civilization, beauty, history! Surprising
turnings of streets, shapes of venerable cottages, lovely
aged eaves, unexpected and gossamer turrets, steeples,
the gloss, the antiquity! Gardens. Whoever speaks of
Paris has never seen Warsaw. Her father, like her
mother, mocked at Yiddish; there was not a particle of
ghetto left in him, not a grain of rot. Whoever yearns
for an aristocratic sensibility, let him switch on the
great light of Warsaw.

'Your name?' her companion said.

'Lublin, Rosa.'

'A pleasure,' he said. 'Only why backwards? I'm an application form? Very good. You apply, I accept.' He took command of her shopping cart. 'Wherever is your home is my direction that I'm going anyhow.'

'You forgot to take your laundry,' Rosa said.

'Mine I did day before yesterday.'

'So why did you come here?'

'I'm devoted to Nature. I like the sound of a waterfall. Wherever it's cool it's a pleasure to sit and read my paper.'

'What a story!' Rosa snorted.

'All right, so I go to have a visit with the ladies. Tell me, you like concerts?'

'I like my own room, that's all.'

'A lady what wants to be a hermit!'

'I got my own troubles,' Rosa said.

'Unload on me.'

In the street she plodded beside him dumbly; a led animal. Her shoes were not nice, she should have put on the other ones. The sunlight was smothering – cooked honey dumped on their heads: one lick was good, too much could drown you. She was glad to have someone to pull the cart.

'You got internal warnings about talking to a stranger? If I say my name, no more a stranger. Simon

Persky. A third cousin to Shimon Peres, the Israeli politician. I have different famous relatives, plenty of family pride. You ever heard of Betty Bacall, who Humphrey Bogard the movie star was married to, a Jewish girl? Also a distant cousin. I could tell you the whole story of my life experience, beginning with Warsaw. Actually it wasn't Warsaw, it was a little place a few miles out of town. In Warsaw I had uncles.'

Rosa said again, 'Your Warsaw isn't my Warsaw.'

He stopped the cart. 'What is this? A song with one stanza? You think I don't know the difference between generations? I'm seventy-one, and you, you're only a girl.'

'Fifty-eight.' Though in the papers, when they told how she smashed up her store, it came out fifty-nine. Stella's fault, Stella's black will, the Angel of Death's arithmetic.

'You see? I told you! A girl!'

'I'm from an educated family.'

'Your English ain't better than what any other refugee talks.'

'Why should I learn English? I didn't ask for it, I got nothing to do with it.'

'You can't live in the past,' he advised. Again the wheels of the cart were squealing. Like a calf, Rosa followed. They were approaching a self-service cafeteria. The smells of eggplant, fried potatoes, mushrooms, blew out as if pumped. Rosa read the sign:

KOLLINS KOSHER KAMEO:
EVERYTHING ON YOUR PLATE AS PRETTY AS A PICTURE:
REMEMBRANCES OF NEW YORK AND THE
PARADISE OF YOUR MATERNAL KITCHEN:
DELICIOUS DISHES OF AMBROSIA AND NOSTALGIA:
AIR CONDITIONED THRU-OUT

'I know the owner,' Persky said. 'He's a big reader. You want tea?'

'Tea?'

'Not iced. The hotter the better. This is physiology. Come in, you'll cool off. You got some red face, believe me.'

Rosa looked in the window. Her bun was loose, strings dangling on either side of her neck. The reflection of a ragged old bird with worn feathers. Skinny, a stork. Her dress was missing a button, but maybe the belt buckle covered this shame. What did she care? She thought of her room, her bed, her radio. She hated conversation.

'I got to get back,' she said.

'An appointment?'

'No.'

'Then have an appointment with Persky. So come, first tea. If you take with an ice cube, you're involved in a mistake.'

They went in and chose a tiny table in a corner – a sticky disk on a wobbly plastic pedestal. 'You'll stay, I'll get,' Persky said.

She sat and panted. Silverware tapped and clicked

all around. No one here but old people. It was like the dining room of a convalescent home. Everyone had canes, dowager's humps, acrylic teeth, shoes cut out for bunions. Everyone wore an open collar showing mottled skin, ferocious clavicles, the wrinkled foundations of wasted breasts. The air-conditioning was on too high; she felt the cooling sweat licking from around her neck down, down her spine into the crevice of her bottom. She was afraid to shift; the chair had a wicker back and a black plastic seat. If she moved even a little, an odor would fly up: urine, salt, old woman's fatigue. She left off panting and shivered. What do I care? I'm used to everything. Florida, New York, it doesn't matter. All the same, she took out two hairpins and caught up the hanging strands; she shoved them into the core of her gray knot and pierced them through. She had no mirror, no comb, no pocketbook; not even a handkerchief. All she had was a Kleenex pushed into her sleeve and some coins in the pocket of her dress.

'I came out only for the laundry,' she told Persky – with a groan he set down a loaded tray: two cups of tea, a saucer of lemon slices, a dish of eggplant salad, bread on what looked like a wooden platter but was really plastic, another plastic platter of Danish. 'Maybe I didn't bring enough to pay.'

'Never mind, you got the company of a rich retired taxpayer. I'm a well-off man. When I get my Social Security, I spit on it.'

'What line of business?'

'The same what I see you got one lost. At the waist. Buttons. A shame. That kind's hard to match, as far as I'm concerned we stopped making them around a dozen years ago. Braided buttons is out of style.'

'Buttons?' Rosa said.

'Buttons, belts, notions, knickknacks, costume jewelry. A factory. I thought my son would take it over but he wanted something different. He's a philosopher, so he became a loiterer. Too much education makes fools. I hate to say it, but on account of him I had to sell out. And the girls, whatever the big one wanted, the little one also. The big one found a lawyer, that's what the little one looked for. I got one son-in-law in business for himself, taxes, the other's a youngster, still on Wall Street.'

'A nice family,' Rosa bit off.

'A loiterer's not so nice. Drink while it's hot. Otherwise it won't reach to your metabolism. You like eggplant salad on top of bread and butter? You got room for it, rest assured. Tell me, you live alone?'

'By myself,' Rosa said, and slid her tongue into the tea. Tears came from the heat.

'My son is over thirty, I still support him.'

'My niece, forty-nine, not married, she supports me.'

'Too old. Otherwise I'd say let's make a match with my son, let her support him too. The best thing is independence. If you're able-bodied, it's a blessing to work.' Persky caressed his chest. 'I got a bum heart.'

Rosa murmured, 'I had a business, but I broke it up.'

'Bankruptcy?'

'Part with a big hammer,' she said meditatively, 'part with a piece of construction metal I picked up from the gutter.'

'You don't look that strong. Skin and bones.'

'You don't believe me? In the papers they said an ax, but where would I get an ax?'

'That's reasonable. Where would you get an ax?' Persky's finger removed an obstruction from under his lower plate. He examined it: an eggplant seed. On the floor near the cart there was something white, a white cloth. Handkerchief. He picked it up and stuffed it in his pants pocket. Then he said, 'What kind of business?'

'Antiques. Old furniture. Junk. I had a specialty in antique mirrors. Whatever I had there, I smashed it. See,' she said, '*now* you're sorry you started with me!'

'I ain't sorry for nothing,' Persky said. 'If there's one thing I know to understand, it's mental episodes. I got it my whole life with my wife.'

'You're not a widower?'

'In a manner of speaking.'

'Where is she?'

'Great Neck, Long Island. A private hospital, it don't cost me peanuts.' He said, 'She's in a mental condition.'

'Serious?'

'It used to be once in a while, now it's a regular thing. She's mixed up that she's somebody else.

33

Television stars. Movie actresses. Different people. Lately my cousin, Betty Bacall. It went to her head.'

'Tragic,' Rosa said.

'You see? I unloaded on you, now you got to unload on me.'

'Whatever I would say, you would be deaf.'

'How come you smashed up your business?'

'It was a store. I didn't like who came in it.'

'Spanish? Colored?'

'What do I care who came? Whoever came, they were like deaf people. Whatever you explained to them, they didn't understand.' Rosa stood up to claim her cart. 'It's very fine of you to treat me to the Danish, Mr Persky. I enjoyed it. Now I got to go.'

'I'll walk you.'

'No, no, sometimes a person feels to be alone.'

'If you're alone too much,' Persky said, 'you think too much.'

'Without a life,' Rosa answered, 'a person lives where they can. If all they got is thoughts, that's where they live.'

'You ain't got a life?'

'Thieves took it.'

She toiled away from him. The handle of the cart was a burning rod. A hat, I ought to have worn a hat! The pins in her bun scalded her scalp. She panted like a dog in the sun. Even the trees looked exhausted: every leaf face downward under a powder of dust. Summer without end, a mistake!

In the lobby she waited before the elevator. The 'guests' – some had been residents for a dozen years – were already milling around, groomed for lunch, the old women in sundresses showing their thick collarbones and the bluish wells above them. Instead of napes they had rolls of wide fat. They wore no stockings. Brazen blue-marbled sinews strangled their squarish calves; in their reveries they were again young women with immortal pillar legs, the white legs of strong goddesses; it was only that they had forgotten about impermanence. In their faces, too, you could see everything they were not noticing about themselves – the red gloss on their drawstring mouths was never meant to restore youth. It was meant only to continue it. Flirts of seventy. Everything had stayed the same for them: intentions, actions, even expectations – they had not advanced. They believed in the seamless continuity of the body. The men were more inward, running their lives in front of their eyes like secret movies.

A syrup of cologne clogged the air. Rosa heard the tearing of envelopes, the wing-shudders of paper sheets. Letters from children: the guests laughed and wept, but without seriousness, without belief. Report-card marks, separations, divorces, a new coffee table to match the gilt mirror over the piano, Stuie at sixteen learning to drive, Millie's mother-in-law's second stroke, rumors of the cataracts of half-remembered acquaintances, a cousin's kidney, the rabbi's ulcer, a daughter's indigestion, burglary, perplexing news of East Hampton parties, psychoanalysis . . . the children were rich, how was this possible from such poor parents? It was real and it was not real. Shadows on a wall; the shadows stirred, but you could not penetrate the wall. The guests were detached; they had detached themselves. Little by little they were forgetting their grandchildren, their aging children. More and more they were growing significant to themselves. Every wall of the lobby a mirror. Every mirror hanging thirty years. Every table surface a mirror. In these mirrors the guests appeared to themselves as they used to be, powerful women of thirty, striving fathers of thirty-five, mothers and fathers of dim children who had migrated long ago, to other continents, inaccessible landscapes, incomprehensible vocabularies. Rosa made herself brave; the elevator gate opened, but she let the empty car ascend without her and pushed the cart through to where the black Cuban receptionist sat, maneuvering clayey sweat balls up from the naked place between her breasts with two fingers.

'Mail for Lublin, Rosa,' Rosa said.

'Lublin, you lucky today. Two letters.'

'Take a look where you keep packages also.'

'You a lucky dog, Lublin,' the Cuban girl said, and tossed an object into the pile of wash.

Rosa knew what was in that package. She had asked Stella to send it; Stella did not easily do what Rosa asked. She saw immediately that the package was not registered. This angered her: Stella the Angel of Death! Instantly she plucked the package out of the cart and tore the wrapping off and crumpled it into a standing ashtray. Magda's shawl! Suppose, God forbid, it got lost in the mail, what then? She squashed the box into her breasts. It felt hard, heavy; Stella had encased it in some terrible untender rind; Stella had turned it to stone. She wanted to kiss it, but the maelstrom was all around her, pressing toward the dining room. The food was monotonous and sparse and often stale; still, to eat there increased the rent. Stella was all the time writing that she was not a millionaire; Rosa never ate in the dining room. She kept the package tight against her bosom and picked through the crowd, a sluggish bird on ragged toes, dragging the cart.

In her room she breathed noisily, almost a gasp, almost a squeal, left the laundry askew in the tiny parody of a vestibule, and carried the box and the two letters to the bed. It was still unmade, fish-smelling, the covers knotted together like an umbilical cord. A shipwreck. She let herself down into it and knocked off her shoes – oh, they were scarred; that Persky must have seen her shame, first the missing button, afterward the used-up shoes. She turned the box round and round – a rectangular box. Magda's shawl! Magda's swaddling cloth. Magda's shroud. The memory of Magda's smell, the holy fragrance of the lost babe. Murdered. Thrown against the fence, barbed, thorned, electrified; grid and griddle; a furnace, the child on fire! Rosa put the shawl to her nose, to her lips. Stella did not want her to have Magda's shawl all the time; she had such funny names for having it – trauma, fetish, God knows what: Stella took psychology courses at the New School at night, looking for marriage among the flatulent bachelors in her classes.

One letter was from Stella and the other was one of those university letters, still another one, another sample of the disease. But in the box, Magda's shawl! The box would be last, Stella's fat letter first (fat meant trouble), the university letter did not matter. A disease. Better to put away the laundry than to open the university letter.

Dear Rosa [Stella wrote]:

All right, I've done it. Been to the post office and mailed it. Your idol is on its way, separate cover. Go on your knees to it if you want. You make yourself crazy, everyone thinks you're a crazy woman. Whoever goes by your old store still gets glass in their soles. You're the older one, I'm the niece, I shouldn't lecture, but my God! It's thirty years, forty, who knows, give it a rest. It isn't as if I don't know just exactly how you do it, what it's like. What a scene, disgusting! You'll open the box and take it out and cry, and you'll kiss it like a crazy person. Making holes in it with kisses. You're like those people in the Middle Ages who worshiped a piece of the True Cross, a splinter from some old outhouse as far as anybody knew, or else they fell down in front of a single hair supposed to be some saint's. You'll kiss, you'll pee tears down your face, and so what? Rosa, by now, believe me, it's time, you have to have a life.

Out loud Rosa said: 'Thieves took it.'
And she said: 'And you, Stella, *you* have a life?'

If I were a millionaire I'd tell you the same thing: get a job. Or else, come back and move in here. I'm away the whole day, it will be like living alone if that's what you want. It's too hot to look around down there, people get like vegetables. With everything you did for me I don't mind keeping up this way maybe another year or so, you'll think I'm stingy for saying it like that, but after all I'm not on the biggest salary in the world.

Rosa said, 'Stella! Would you be alive if I didn't take you out from there? Dead. You'd be dead! So don't talk to me how much an old woman costs! I didn't give you from my store? The big gold mirror, you look in it at your bitter face – I don't care how pretty, even so it's bitter – and you forget who gave you presents!'

And as far as Florida is concerned, well, it doesn't solve anything. I don't mind telling you now that they would have locked you up if I didn't agree to get you out of the city then and there. One more public outburst puts you in the bughouse. No more public scandals! For God's sake, don't be a crazy person! Live your life!

Rosa said again, 'Thieves took it,' and went, scrupulously, meticulously, as if possessed, to count the laundry in the cart.

A pair of underpants was missing. Once more Rosa counted everything: four blouses, three cotton skirts, three brassieres, one half-slip and one regular, two towels, eight pairs of underpants . . . nine went into the washing machine, the exact number. Degrading. Lost bloomers – dropped God knows where. In the elevator, in the lobby, in the street even. Rosa tugged, and the dress with the blue stripes slid like a coarse colored worm out of twisted bedsheets. The hole in the armpit was bigger now. Stripes, never again anything on her body with stripes! She swore it, but this, fancy and with a low collar, was Stella's birthday present, Stella bought it. As if innocent, as if ignorant, as if *not there*. Stella, an ordinary American, indistinguishable! No one could guess what hell she had crawled out of until she opened her mouth and up coiled the smoke of accent.

Again Rosa counted. A fact, one pair of pants lost. An old woman who couldn't even hang on to her own underwear.

She decided to sew up the hole in the stripes. Instead she put water on to boil for tea and made the bed with the clean sheets from the cart. The box with the shawl would be the last thing. Stella's letter she pushed under the bed next to the telephone. She tidied all around. Everything had to be nice when the box was opened. She spread jelly on three crackers and deposited a Lipton's teabag on the Welch's lid. It was grape jelly, with a picture of Bugs Bunny elevating an officious finger. In spite of Persky's Danish, empty insides. Always Stella said: Rosa eats little by little, like a tapeworm in the world's belly.

Then it came to her that Persky had her underpants in his pocket.

Oh, degrading. The shame. Pain in the loins. Burning. Bending in the cafeteria to pick up her pants, all the while tinkering with his teeth. Why didn't he give them back? He was embarrassed. He had thought a handker-chief. How can a man hand a woman, a stranger, a piece of her own underwear? He could have shoved it right back into the cart, how would that look? A sensitive man, he wanted to spare her. When he came home with her underpants, what then? What could a man, half a widower, do with a pair of female bloomers? Nylon-plus-cotton, the long-thighed kind. Maybe he had filched them on purpose, a sex maniac, a wife among the insane, his parts starved. According to Stella, Rosa also belonged among the insane, Stella had the power to put her there. Very good, they would become neighbors, confidantes, she and Persky's wife, best friends. The wife would confess all of Persky's sexual habits. She would explain how it is that a man of this age comes to steal a lady's personal underwear.

Whatever stains in the crotch are nobody's business. And not only that: a woman with children, Persky's wife would speak of her son and her married lucky daughters. And Rosa too, never mind how Stella was sour over it, she would tell about Magda, a beautiful young woman of thirty, thirty-one: a doctor married to a doctor; large house in Mamaroneck, New York; two medical offices, one on the first floor, one in the finished basement. Stella was alive, why not Magda? Who was Stella, coarse Stella, to insist that Magda was not alive? Stella the Angel of Death. Magda alive, the pure eyes, the bright hair. Stella, never a mother, who was Stella to mock the kisses Rosa put in Magda's shawl? She meant to crush it into her mouth. Rosa, a mother the same as anyone, no different from Persky's wife in the crazy house.

This disease! The university letter, like all of them – five, six postmarks on the envelope. Rosa imagined its pilgrimage: first to the *News*, the *Post*, maybe even the *Times*, then to Rosa's old store, then to the store's landlord's lawyers, then to Stella's apartment, then to Miami, Florida. A Sherlock Holmes of a letter. It had struggled to find its victim, and for what? More eating alive.

April 17, 1977

Dear Ms Lublin:

Though I am not myself a physician, I have lately begun to amass survivor data as rather a considerable specialty. To be concrete: I am presently working on a study, funded by the Minew Foundation of the Kansas—Iowa Institute for Humanitarian Context, designed to research the theory developed by Dr Arthur R. Hidgeson and known generally as Repressed Animation. Without at this stage going into detail, it may be of some preliminary use to you to know that investigations so far reveal an astonishing generalized minimalization during any extended period of stress resulting from incarceration, exposure, and malnutrition. We have turned up a wide range of neurological residues (including, in some cases, acute cerebral damage, derangement, disorientation, premature senility, etc.), as well as hormonal changes, parasites, anemia, thready pulse, hyperventilation, etc.; in children especially, temperatures as high as 108°, ascitic fluid, retardation, bleeding sores on the skin and in the mouth, etc. What is remarkable is that these are all *current conditions* in survivors and their families.

Disease, disease! Humanitarian Context, what did it mean? An excitement over other people's suffering. They let their mouths water up. Stories about children running blood in America from sores, what muck. Consider also the special word they used: *survivor*.

Something new. As long as they didn't have to say *human being*. It used to be *refugee*, but by now there was no such creature, no more refugees, only survivors. A name like a number – counted apart from the ordinary swarm. Blue digits on the arm, what difference? They don't call you a woman anyhow. *Survivor*. Even when your bones get melted into the grains of the earth, still they'll forget *human being*. Survivor and survivor and survivor; always and always. Who made up these words, parasites on the throat of suffering!

For some months teams of medical paraphrasers have been conducting interviews with survivors, to contrast current medical paraphrase with conditions found more than three decades ago, at the opening of the camps. This, I confess, is neither my field nor my interest. My own concern, both as a scholar of social pathology and as a human being . . .

Ha! For himself it was good enough, for himself he didn't forget this word *human being*!

. . . is not with medical nor even with psychological aspects of survivor data.

Data. Drop in a hole!

What particularly engages me for purposes of my own participation in the study (which, by the way, is intended to be definitive, to close the books, so to speak, on this lamentable subject) is what I can only term the 'metaphysical' side of Repressed Animation (R.A.). It begins to be evident that prisoners gradually came to Buddhist positions. They gave up craving and began to function in terms of non-functioning, i.e., non-attachment. The Four Noble Truths in Buddhist thought, if I may remind you, yield a penetrating summary of the fruit of craving: pain. 'Pain' in this view is defined as ugliness, age, sorrow, sickness, despair, and, finally, birth. Non-attachment is attained through the Eightfold Path, the highest stage of which is the cessation of all human craving, the loftiest rapture, one might say, of consummated in-difference.

It is my hope that these speculations are not displeasing to you. Indeed, I further hope that they may even attract you, and that you would not object to joining our study by means of an in-depth interview to be conducted by me at, if it is not inconvenient, your home. I should like to observe survivor syndroming within the natural setting.

Home. Where, where?

As you may not realize, the national convention of the American Association of Clinical Social Pathology has this year, for reasons of fairness to our East Coast members, been moved from Las Vegas to Miami Beach. The convention will take place at a hotel in your vicinity about the middle of next May, and I would be deeply grateful if you could receive me during that period. I have noted via a New York City newspaper (we are not so provincial out here as some may think!) your recent removal to Florida; consequently you are ideally circumstanced to make a contribution to our R.A. study. I look forward to your consent at your earliest opportunity.

Very sincerely yours,
James W. Tree, Ph.D.

Drop in a hole! Disease! It comes from Stella, everything! Stella saw what this letter was, she could see from the envelope – Dr Stella! Kansas–Iowa Clinical Social Pathology, a fancy hotel, this is the cure for the taking of a life! Angel of Death!

With these university letters Rosa had a routine: she carried the scissors over to the toilet bowl and snipped little bits of paper and flushed. In the bowl going down, the paper squares whirled like wedding rice.

But this one: drop in a hole with your Four Truths and your Eight Paths together! Non-attachment! She threw the letter into the sink; also its crowded envelope ('Please forward', Stella's handwriting instructed, pretending to be American, leaving out the little stroke that goes across the 7); she lit a match and enjoyed the thick fire. Burn, Dr Tree, burn up with your Repressed Animation! The world is full of Trees! The world is full of fire! Everything, everything is on fire! Florida is burning!

Big flakes of cinder lay in the sink: black foliage, Stella's black will. Rosa turned on the faucet and the cinders spiraled down and away. Then she went to the round oak table and wrote the first letter of the day to her daughter, her healthy daughter, her daughter who suffered neither from thready pulse nor from anemia, her daughter who was a professor of Greek philosophy at Columbia University in New York City, a stone's throw – the philosopher's stone that prolongs life and transmutes iron to gold – from Stella in Queens!

Magda, my Soul's Blessing [Rosa wrote]:

Forgive me, my yellow lioness. Too long a time since the last writing. Strangers scratch at my life; they pursue, they break down the bloodstream's sentries. Always there is Stella. And so half a day passes without my taking up my pen to speak to you. A pleasure, the deepest pleasure, home bliss, to speak in our own language. Only to you. I am always having to write to Stella now, like a dog paying respects to its mistress. It's my obligation. She sends me money. She, whom I plucked out of the claws of all those Societies that came to us with bread and chocolate after the liberation! Despite everything, they were selling sectarian ideas; collecting troops for their armies. If not for me they would have shipped Stella with a boatload of orphans to Palestine, to become God knows what, to live God knows how. A field worker jabbering Hebrew. It would serve her right. Americanized airs. My father was never a Zionist. He used to call himself a 'Pole by right'. The Jews, he said, didn't put a thousand years of brains and blood into Polish soil in order to have to prove themselves to anyone. He was the wrong sort of idealist, maybe, but he had the instincts of a natural nobleman. I could laugh at that now – the whole business – but I don't, because I feel too vividly what he was, how substantial, how not given over to any light-mindedness whatever. He had Zionist friends in his youth. Some left Poland early and lived. One is a bookseller in Tel Aviv. He specializes in foreign texts and periodicals. My poor little father. It's only history – an ad hoc instance of it, you might say – that made the Zionist answer. My father's ideas were more logical. He was a Polish patriot on a temporary basis, he said, until the time when nation should lie down beside nation like the lily and the lotus. He was at bottom a prophetic creature. My mother, you know, published poetry. To you all these accounts must have the ring of pure legend.

Even Stella, who *can* remember, refuses. She calls me a parable-maker. She was always jealous of you. She has a strain of dementia, and resists you and all other reality. Every vestige of former existence is an insult to her. Because she fears the past she distrusts the future – it, too, will turn into the past. As a result she has nothing. She sits and watches the present roll itself up into the past more quickly than she can bear. That's why she never found the one thing she wanted more than anything, an American husband. I'm immune to these pains and panics. Motherhood – I've always known this – is a profound distraction from philo-sophy, and all philosophy is rooted in suffering over the passage of time. I mean the *fact* of motherhood, the physio-logical fact. To have the power to create another human being, to be the instrument of such a mystery. To pass on a whole genetic system. I don't believe in God, but I believe, like the Catholics, in mystery. My mother wanted so much to convert; my father laughed at her. But she was attracted. She let the maid keep a statue of the Virgin and Child in the corner of the kitchen. Sometimes she used to go in and look at it. I can even remember the words of a poem she wrote about the heat coming up from the stove, from the Sunday pancakes —

> Mother of God, how you shiver
> in these heat-ribbons!
> Our cakes rise to you
> and in the trance of His birthing
> you hide.

Something like that. Better than that, more remarkable. Her Polish was very dense. You had to open it out like a fan to get at all the meanings. She was exceptionally modest, but she was not afraid to call herself a symbolist.

I know you won't blame me for going astray with such tales. After all, you're always prodding me for these old memories. If not for you, I would have buried them all, to satisfy Stella. Stella Columbus! She thinks there's such a thing as the New World, Finally — at last, at last — she surrenders this precious vestige of your sacred babyhood. Here it is in a box right next to me as I write. She didn't take the trouble to send it by registered mail! Even though I told her and told her. I've thrown out the wrapping paper, and the lid is plastered down with lots of Scotch tape. I'm not hurrying to open it. At first my hunger was unrestrained and I couldn't wait, but nothing is nice now. I'm saving you; I want to be serene. In a state of agitation one doesn't split open a diamond. Stella says I make a relic of you. She has no heart. It would shock you if I told you even one of the horrible games I'm made to play with her. To soothe her dementia, to keep her quiet, I pretend you died. Yes! It's true! There's nothing, however crazy, I wouldn't say to her to tie up her tongue. She slanders. Everywhere there are slanders, and sometimes – my bright lips, my darling! – the slanders touch even you. My purity, my snowqueen!

I'm ashamed to give an example. Pornography. What Stella, that pornographer, has made of your father. She thieves all the truth, she robs it, she steals it, the robbery goes unpunished. She lies, and it's the lying that's rewarded. The New World! That's why I smashed up my store! Because here they make up lying theories. University people do the same: they take human beings for specimens. In Poland there used to be justice; here they have social theories. Their system inherits almost nothing from the Romans, that's why. Is it a wonder that the lawyers are no better than scavengers who feed on the droppings of thieves and liars? Thank God you followed your grandfather's bent and studied philosophy and not law.

Take my word for it, Magda, your father and I had the most ordinary lives – by 'ordinary' I mean respectable, gentle, cultivated. Reliable people of refined reputation. His name was Andrzej. Our families had status. Your father was the son of my mother's closest friend. She was a converted Jew married to a Gentile: you can be a Jew if you like, or a Gentile, it's up to you. You have a legacy of choice, and they say choice is the only true freedom. We were engaged to be married. We would have been married. Stella's accusations are all Stella's own excretion. Your father was not a German. I was forced by a German, it's true, and more than once, but I was too sick to conceive. Stella has a naturally pornographic mind, she can't resist dreaming up a dirty sire for you, an S.S. man! Stella was with me the whole time, she knows just what

I know. They never put me in their brothel either. Never believe this, my lioness, my snowqueen! No lies come out of me to you. You are pure. A mother is the source of consciousness, of conscience, the ground of being, as philosophers say. I have no falsehoods for you. Otherwise I don't deny some few tricks: the necessary handful. To those who don't deserve the truth, don't give it. I tell Stella what it pleases her to hear. My child, perished. Perished. She always wanted it. She was always jealous of you. She has no heart. Even now she believes in my loss of you: and you a stone's throw from her door in New York! Let her think whatever she thinks; her mind is awry, poor thing; in me the strength of your being consumes my joy. Yellow blossom! Cup of the sun!

What a curiosity it was to hold a pen – nothing but a small pointed stick, after all, oozing its hieroglyphic puddles: a pen that speaks, miraculously, Polish. A lock removed from the tongue. Otherwise the tongue is chained to the teeth and the palate. An immersion into the living language: all at once this cleanliness, this capacity, this power to make a history, to tell, to explain. To retrieve, to reprieve!

To lie.

The box with Magda's shawl was still on the table. Rosa left it there. She put on her good shoes, a nice dress (polyester, 'wrinkle-free' on the inside label); she arranged her hair, brushed her teeth, poured mouthwash on the brush, sucked it up through the nylon bristles, gargled rapidly. As an afterthought she changed her bra and slip; it meant getting out of her dress and into it again. Her mouth she reddened very slightly – a smudge of lipstick rubbed on with a finger.

Perfected, she mounted the bed on her knees and fell into folds. A puppet, dreaming. Darkened cities, tombstones, colorless garlands, a black fire in a gray field, brutes forcing the innocent, women with their mouths stretched and their arms wild, her mother's voice calling. After hours of these pitiless tableaux, it was late afternoon; by then she was certain that whoever put her underpants in his pocket was a criminal capable of every base act. Humiliation. Degradation. Stella's pornography!

To retrieve, to reprieve. Nothing in the elevator; in the lobby, nothing. She kept her head down. Nothing white glimmered up.

In the street, a neon dusk was already blinking. Gritty mixture of heat and toiling dust. Cars shot by like large bees. It was too early for headlights: in the lower sky two strange competing lamps – a scarlet sun, round and brilliant as a blooded egg yolk; a silk-white moon, gray-veined with mountain ranges. These hung simultaneously at either end of the long road. The whole day's burning struck upward like a moving weight from the sidewalk. Rosa's nostrils and lungs were cautious: burning molasses air. Her underpants were not in the road.

In Miami at night no one stays indoors. The streets are clogged with wanderers and watchers; everyone in search, bedouins with no fixed paths. The foolish Florida rains spray down – so light, so brief and fickle, no one pays attention. Neon alphabets, designs, pictures, flashing undiminished right through the sudden small rain. A quick lick of lightning above one of the balconied hotels. Rosa walked. Much Yiddish. Caravans of slow old couples, linked at the elbows, winding down to the cool of the beaches. The sand never at rest, always churning, always inhabited; copulation under blankets at night, beneath neon-radiant low horizons.

She had never been near the beach; why should her underpants be lost in the sand?

On the sidewalk in front of the Kollins Kosher Kameo, nothing. Shining hungry smell of boiled potatoes in soured cream. The pants were not necessarily in Persky's pocket. Dented garbage barrels, empty near the curb. Pants already smouldering in an ash heap, among blackened tomato cans, kitchen scrapings, conflagrations of old magazines. Or: a simple omission, an accident, never transferred from the washing machine to the dryer. Or, if transferred, never removed. Overlooked. Persky unblemished. The laundromat was locked up for the night, with a metal accordion gate stretched across the door and windows. What marauders would seek out caldrons, giant washtubs? Property misleads, brings false perspectives. The power to smash her own. A kind of suicide. She had murdered her store with her own hands. She cared more for a missing pair of underpants, lost laundry, than for business. She was ashamed; she felt exposed. What was her store? A cave of junk.

On the corner across the street from the laundromat, a narrow newspaper store, no larger than a stall. Persky might have bought his paper there. Suppose later in the day he had come down for an afternoon paper, her pants in his pocket, and dropped them?

Mob of New York accents. It was a little place, not air-conditioned.

'Lady? You're looking for something?'

A newspaper? Rosa had enough of the world.

'Look, it's like sardines in here, buy something or go out.'

'My store used to be six times the size of this place,' Rosa said.

'So go to your store.'

'I don't have a store.' She reconsidered. If someone wanted to hide – to hide, not destroy – a pair of underpants, where would he put them? Under the sand. Rolled up and buried. She thought what a weight of sand would feel like in the crotch of her pants, wet heavy sand, still hot from the day. In her room it was hot, hot all night. No air. In Florida there was no air, only this syrup seeping into the esophagus. Rosa walked; she saw everything, but as if out of invention, out of imagination; she was unconnected to anything. She came to a gate; a mottled beach spread behind it. It belonged to one of the big hotels. The latch opened. At the edge of the waves you could look back and see black crenellated forms stretching all along the shore. In the dark, in silhouette, the towered hotel roofs held up their merciless teeth. Impossible that any architect pleasurably dreamed these teeth. The sand was only now beginning to cool. Across the water the sky breathed a starless black; behind her, where the hotels bit down on the city, a dusty glow of brownish red lowered. Mud clouds. The sand was littered with bodies. Photograph of Pompeii: prone in the volcanic ash. Her pants were under the sand; or else packed hard with sand, like a piece of torso, a broken statue, the human groin detached, the whole soul gone, only the loins left for kicking by strangers. She took off her good shoes to save them and nearly stepped on the sweated faces of two lovers plugged into a kiss. A pair of water animals in suction. The same everywhere, along the rim of every continent, this gurgling, foaming, trickling A true smasher, a woman whose underpants have been stolen, a woman who has murdered her business with her own hands, would know how to step cleanly into the sea. A horizontal tunnel. You can fall into its pull just by entering it upright. How simple the night sea; only the sand is unpredictable, with its hundred burrowings, its thousand buryings.

When she came back to the gate, the latch would not budge. A cunning design, it trapped the trespasser.

She gazed up, and thought of climbing; but there

was barbed wire on top.

So many double mounds in the sand. It was a question of choosing a likely sentinel: someone who would let her out. She went back down onto the beach again and tapped a body with the tip of her dangling shoe. The body jerked as if shot: it scrambled up.

'Mister? You know how to get out?'

'Room key does it,' said the second body, still flat in the sand. It was a man. They were both men, slim and coated with sand; naked. The one lying flat – she could see what part of him was swollen.

'I'm not from this hotel,' Rosa said.

'Then you're not allowed here. This is a private beach.'

'Can't you let me out?'

'Lady, please. Just buzz off,' the man in the sand said.

'I can't get out,' Rosa pleaded.

The man who was standing laughed.

Rosa persisted, 'If you have a key – '

'Believe me, lady, not for you' – muffled from below.

She understood. Sexual mockery. 'Sodom!' she hissed, and stumbled away. Behind her their laughter. They hated women. Or else they saw she was a Jew; they hated Jews; but no, she had noticed the circumcision, like a jonquil, in the dim sand. Her wrists were trembling. To be locked behind barbed wire! No one knew who she was; what had happened to her; where she came from. Their gates, the terrible ruse of their keys, wire brambles, men lying with men . . . She was afraid to approach any of the other mounds. No one to help. Persecutors. In the morning they would arrest her.

She put on her shoes again, and walked along the cement path that followed the fence. It led her to light; voices of black men. A window. Vast deep odors: kitchen exhaust, fans stirring soup smells out into the weeds. A door wedged open by a milk-can lid. Acres of counters, stoves, steamers, refrigerators, percolators, bins, basins. The kitchen of a castle. She fled past the black cooks in their meat-blooded aprons, through a short corridor: a dead end facing an elevator. She pushed the button and waited. The kitchen people had seen her; would they pursue? She heard their yells, but it was nothing to do with her – they were calling Thursday, Thursday. On Thursday no more new potatoes. A kind of emergency maybe. The elevator took her to the main floor, to the lobby; she emerged, free.

This lobby was the hall of a palace. In the middle a real fountain. Water springing out of the mouths of emerald-green dolphins. Skirted cherubs, gilded. A winged mermaid spilling gold flowers out of a gold pitcher. Lofty plants – a forest – palms sprayed dark blue and silver and gold, leafing out of masses of green marble vessels at the lip of the fountain. The water flowed into a marble channel, a little indoor brook. A royal carpet for miles around, woven with crowned birds. Well-dressed men and women sat in lion-clawed gold thrones, smoking. A golden babble. How happy Stella would be, to stroll in a place like this! Rosa kept close to the walls.

She saw a man in a green uniform.

'The manager,' she croaked. 'I have to tell him something.'

'Office is over there.' He shrugged toward a mahogany desk behind a glass wall. The manager, wearing a red wig, was making a serious mark on a crested letterhead. Persky, too, had a red wig. Florida was glutted with fake fire, burning false hair! Everyone a piece of imposter. 'Ma'am?' the manager said.

'Mister, you got barbed wire by your beach.'

'Are you a guest here?'

'I'm someplace else.'

'Then it's none of your business, is it?'

'You got barbed wire.'

'It keeps out the riffraff.'

'In America it's no place for barbed wire on top of fences.'

The manager left off making his serious marks. 'Will you leave?' he said. 'Will you please just leave?'

'Only Nazis catch innocent people behind barbed wire,' Rosa said.

The red wig dipped. 'My name is Finkelstein.'

'Then you should know better!'

'Listen, walk out of here if you know what's good for you.'

'Where were you when we was there?'

'Get out. So far I'm asking nicely. Please get out.'

'Dancing in the pool by the lobby, that's where. Eat your barbed wire, Mr Finkelstein, chew it and choke on it!'

'Go home,' Finkelstein said.

'You got Sodom and Gomorrah in your back yard! You got gays and you got barbed wire!'

'You were trespassing on our beach,' the manager said. 'You want me to call the police? Better leave before. Some important guests have come in, we can't tolerate the noise, and I can't spare the time for this.'

'They write me letters all the time, your important guests. Conventions,' Rosa scoffed. 'Clinical Social Pathology, right? You got a Dr Tree staying?'

'Please go,' Finkelstein said.

'Come on, you got a Dr Tree? No? I'll tell you, if not today you'll get him later on, he's on the way. He's coming to investigate specimens. I'm the important one! It's me he's interviewing. Finkelstein, not you! I'm the study!'

The red wig dipped again.

'Aha!' Rosa cried. 'I see you got Tree! You got a whole bunch of Trees!'

'We protect the privacy of our guests.'

'With barbed wire you protect. It's Tree, yes? I can see I'm right! It's Tree! You got Tree staying here, right? Admit you got Tree! Finkelstein, you S.S., admit it!'

The manager stood up. 'Out,' he said. 'Get out now. Immediately.'

'Don't worry, it's all right. It's my business to keep away. Tree I don't need. With Trees I had enough, you don't have to concern yourself – '

'*Leave*,' said the red wig.

'A shame,' Rosa said, 'a Finkelstein like you.' Irradiated, triumphant, cleansed, Rosa marched through the emerald glitter, toward the illuminated marquee in front. HOTEL MARIE LOUISE, in green neon. A doorman like a British admiral, gold braid cascading from his shoulders. They had trapped her, nearly caught her; but she knew how to escape. Speak up, yell. The same way she saved Stella, when they were pressing to take her on the boat to Palestine. She had no fear of Jews; sometimes she had – it came from her mother, her father – a certain contempt. The Warsaw swarm, shut off from the grandeur of the true world. Neighborhoods of a particular kind. Persky and Finkelstein. 'Their' synagogues – balconies for the women. Primitive. Her own home, her own upbringing – how she had fallen. A loathsome tale of folk-sorcery: nobility turned into a small dun rodent. Cracking her teeth on the poison of English. Here they were shallow, they knew nothing. Light-minded. Stella looking, on principle, to be light-minded. Blue stripes, barbed wire, men embracing men . . . whatever was dangerous and repugnant they made prevalent, frivolous.

Lost. Lost. Nowhere. All of Miami Beach, empty;

the sand, empty. The whole wild hot neon night city:
an empty search. In someone's pocket.

Persky was waiting for her. He sat in the torn brown-
plastic wing chair near the reception desk, one leg over
the side, reading a newspaper.

He saw her come in and jumped up. He wore only a
shirt and pants; no tie, no jacket. Informal.

'Lublin, Rosa!'

Rosa said, 'How come you're here?'

'Where you been the whole night? I'm sitting hours.'

'I didn't tell you where I stay,' Rosa accused.

'I looked in the telephone book.'

'My phone's disconnected, I don't know nobody.
My niece, she writes, she saves on long distance.'

'All right. You want the truth? This morning I
followed you, that's all. A simple walk from my place.
I sneaked in the streets behind you. I found out where
you stay, here I am.'

'Very nice,' Rosa said.

'You don't like it?'

She wanted to tell him he was under suspicion; he
owed her a look in his jacket pocket. A self-confessed
sneak who follows women. If not his jacket, his pants.
But it wasn't possible to say a thing like this. Her pants
in his pants. Instead she said, 'What do you want?'

He flashed his teeth. 'A date.'

'You're a married man.'

'A married man what ain't got a wife.'

'You got one.'

'In a manner of speaking. She's crazy.'

Rosa said, 'I'm crazy too.'

'Who says so?'

'My niece.'

'What does a stranger know?'

'A niece isn't a stranger.'

'My own son is a stranger. A niece definitely. Come on, I got my car nearby. Air-conditioned, we'll take a spin.'

'You're not a kid, I'm not a kid,' Rosa said.

'You can't prove it by me,' Persky said.

'I'm a serious person,' Rosa said. 'It isn't my kind of life, to run around noplace.'

'Who said noplace? I got a place in mind.' He considered. 'My Senior Citizens. Very nice pinochle.'

'Not interested,' Rosa said. 'I don't need new people.'

'Then a movie. You don't like new ones, we'll find dead ones. Clark Gable, Jean Harlow.'

'Not interested.'

'A ride to the beach. A walk on the shore, how about it?'

'I already did it,' Rosa said.

'When?'

'Tonight. Just now.'

'Alone?'

Rosa said, 'I was looking for something I lost.'

'Poor Lublin, what did you lose?'

'My life.'

She was all at once not ashamed to say this outright. Because of the missing underwear, she had no dignity before him. She considered Persky's life: how trivial it must always have been: buttons, himself no more significant than a button. It was plain he took her to be another button like himself, battered now and out of fashion, rolled into Florida. All of Miami beach, a box for useless buttons!

'This means you're tired. Tell you what,' Persky said, 'invite me upstairs. A cup of tea. We'll make a conversation. You'll see, I got other ideas up my sleeve – tomorrow we'll go someplace and you'll like it.'

Her room was miraculously ready: tidy, clarified. It was sorted out: you could see where the bed ended and the table commenced. Sometimes it was all one jumble, a highway of confusion. Destiny had clarified her room just in time for a visitor. She started the tea. Persky put his newspaper down on the table, and on top of it an oily paper bag. 'Crullers!' he announced. 'I bought them to eat in the car, but this is very nice, cozy. You got a cozy place, Lublin.'

'Cramped,' Rosa said.

'I work from a different theory. For everything there's a bad way of describing, also a good way. You pick the good way, you get along better.'

'I don't like to give myself lies,' Rosa said.

'Life is short, we all got to lie. Tell me, you got paper

napkins? Never mind, who needs them. Three cups! That's a lucky thing; usually when a person lives alone they don't keep so many. Look, vanilla icing, chocolate icing. Two plain also. You prefer with icing or plain? Such fine tea bags, they got style. Now you see, Lublin? Everything's nice!'

He had set the table. To Rosa this made the corner of the room look new, as if she had never seen it before.

'Don't let the tea cool off. Remember what I told you this morning, the hotter the better,' Persky said; he clanged his spoon happily. 'Here, let's make more elbowroom – '

His hand, greasy from the crullers, was on Magda's box.

'Don't touch!'

'What's the matter? It's something alive in there? A bomb? A rabbit? It's squashable? No, I got it – a lady's hat!'

Rosa hugged the box; she was feeling foolish, trivial. Everything was frivolous here, even the deepest property of being. It seemed to her someone had cut out her life-organs and given them to her to hold. She walked the little distance to the bed – three steps – and set the box down against the pillow. When she turned around, Persky's teeth were persisting in their independent bliss.

'The fact is,' he said, 'I didn't expect nothing from you tonight. You got to work things through, I can see that. You remind me of my son. Even to get a cup of tea from you is worth something, I could do worse. Tomorrow we'll have a real appointment. I'm not inquiring, I'm not requesting. I'll be the boss, what do you say?'

Rosa sat. 'I'm thinking, I should get out and go back to New York to my niece – '

'Not tomorrow. Day after tomorrow you'll change your life, and tomorrow you'll come with me. We got six meetings to pick from.'

Rosa said doubtfully, 'Meetings?'

'Speakers. Lectures for fancy people like yourself. Something higher than pinochle.'

'I don't play,' Rosa acknowledged.

Persky looked around. 'I don't see no books neither. You want me to drive you to the library?'

A thread of gratitude pulled in her throat. He almost understood what she was: no ordinary button. 'I read only Polish,' she told him, 'I don't like to read in English. For literature you need a mother tongue.'

'*Lite*rature, my my. Polish ain't a dime a dozen. It don't grow on trees neither. Lublin, you should adjust. Get used to it!'

She was wary: 'I'm used to everything.'

'Not to being a regular person.'

'My niece Stella,' Rosa slowly gave out, 'says that in America cats have nine lives, but we – we're less than cats, so we got three. The life before, the life during, the life after.' She saw that Persky did not follow. She said, 'The life after is now. The life before is our *real* life, at home, where we was born.'

'And during?'

'This was Hitler.'

'Poor Lublin,' Persky said.

'You wasn't there. From the movies you know it.' She recognized that she had shamed him; she had long ago discovered this power to shame. 'After, after, that's all Stella cares. For me there's one time only; there's no after.'

Persky speculated. 'You want everything the way it was before.'

'No, no, no,' Rosa said. 'It can't be. I don't believe in Stella's cats. Before is a dream. After is a joke. Only during stays. And to call it a life is a lie.'

'But it's over,' Persky said. 'You went through it, now you owe yourself something.'

'This is how Stella talks. Stella – ' Rosa halted; then she came on the word. 'Stella is self-indulgent. She wants to wipe out memory.'

'Sometimes a little forgetting is necessary,' Persky said, 'if you want to get something out of life.'

'Get something! Get *what*?'

'You ain't in a camp. It's finished. Long ago it's finished. Look around, you'll see human beings.'

'What I see,' Rosa said, 'is bloodsuckers.'

Persky hesitated. 'Over there, they took your family?'

Rosa held up all the fingers of her two hands. Then she said: 'I'm left. Stella's left.' She wondered if she dared to tell him more. The box on the bed. 'Out of so many, three.'

Persky asked, 'Three?'

'Evidence,' Rosa said briskly. 'I can show you.'

She raised the box. She felt like a climber on the margin of a precipice. 'Wipe your hands.'

Persky obeyed. He rubbed the last of the cruller crumbs on his shirt front.

'Unpack and look in. Go ahead, lift up what's inside.'

She did not falter. What her own hands longed to do she was yielding to a stranger, a man with pockets; she knew why. To prove herself pure: a madonna. Supposing he had vile old man's thoughts: let him see her with the eye of truth. A mother.

But Persky said, 'How do you count three – '

'Look for yourself.'

He took the cover off and reached into the box and drew out a sheet of paper and began to skim it.

'That has to be from Stella. Throw it out, never mind. More scolding, how I'm a freak – '

'Lublin, you're a regular member of the intelligentsia! This is quite some reading matter. It ain't in Polish neither.' His teeth danced. 'On such a sad subject, allow me a little joke. Who came to America was one, your niece Stella; Lublin, Rosa, this makes two; and Lublin's brain – three!'

Rosa stared. 'I'm a mother, Mr Persky,' she said, 'the same as your wife, no different.' She received the paper between burning palms. 'Have some respect,' she commanded the bewildered glitter of his plastic grin. And read:

Dear Ms Lublin:

I am taking the liberty of sending you, as a token of my good faith, this valuable study by Hidgeson (whom, you may recall, I mentioned in passing in my initial explanatory letter), which more or less lays the ethological groundwork for our current structures. I feel certain that – in preparation for our talks – you will want to take a look at it. A great deal of our work has been built on these phylogenetic insights. You may find some of the language a bit too technical; nevertheless I believe that simply having this volume in your possession will go far toward reassuring you concerning the professionalism of our endeavors, and of your potential contribution toward them.

Of special interest, perhaps, is Chapter Six, entitled 'Defensive Group Formation: The Way of the Baboons.'

Gratefully in advance,

James W. Tree, Ph.D.

Persky said, 'Believe me, I could smell with only one glance it wasn't from Stella.'

She saw that he was holding the thing he had taken out of the box. 'Give me that,' she ordered.

He recited: 'By A. R. Hidgeson. And listen to the title, something fancy – *Repressed Animation: A Theory of the Biological Ground of Survival*. I told you fancy! This isn't what you wanted?'

'Give it to me.'

'You didn't want? Stella sent you what you didn't want?'

'Stella sent!' She tore the book from him – it was heavier than she had guessed – and hurled it at the ceiling. It slammed down into Persky's half-filled teacup. Shards and droplets flew. 'The way I smashed up my store, that's how I'll smash Tree!'

Persky was watching the tea drip to the floor.

'Tree?'

'Dr Tree! Tree the bloodsucker!'

'I can see I'm involved in a mistake,' Persky said. 'I'll tell you what, you eat up the crullers. You'll feel better, and I'll come tomorrow when the mistake is finished.'

'I'm not your button, Persky! I'm nobody's button, not even if they got barbed wire everywhere!'

'Speaking of buttons, I'll go and push the elevator button. Tomorrow I'll come back.'

'Barbed wire! You took my laundry, you think I don't know that? Look in your dirty pockets, you thief Persky!'

In the morning, washing her face – it was swollen, nightmares like weeds, the bulb of her nose pale – Rosa found, curled inside a towel, the missing underwear.

She went downstairs to the desk; she talked over having her phone reconnected. Naturally they would charge more, and Stella would squawk. All the same, she wanted it.

At the desk they handed her a package; this time she examined the wrapping. It had come by registered mail and it was from Stella. It was not possible to be hoodwinked again, but Rosa was shocked, depleted, almost as if yesterday's conflagration hadn't been Tree but really the box with Magda's shawl.

She lifted the lid of the box and looked down at the shawl; she was indifferent. Persky, too, would have been indifferent. The colorless cloth lay like an old bandage; a discarded sling. For some reason it did not instantly restore Magda, as usually happened, a vivid thwack of restoration like an electric jolt. She was willing to wait for the sensation to surge up whenever it would. The shawl had a faint saliva smell, but it was more nearly imagined than smelled.

Under the bed the telephone vibrated: first a sort of buzz, then a real ring. Rosa pulled it out.

The Cuban's voice said: 'Missis Lublin, you connected now.'

Rosa wondered why it was taking so long for Magda to come alive. Sometimes Magda came alive with a brilliant swoop, almost too quickly, so that Rosa's ribs were knocked on their insides by copper hammers, clanging and gonging.

The instrument, still in her grip, drilled again. Rosa started: it was as if she had squeezed a rubber toy. How quickly a dead thing can come to life! Very

tentatively, whispering into a frond, Rosa said, 'Hello?'
It was a lady selling frying pans.

'No,' Rosa said, and dialed Stella. She could hear
that Stella had been asleep. Her throat was softened
by a veil. 'Stella,' Rosa said, 'I'm calling from my
own room.'

'Who is this?'

'Stella, you don't recognize me?'

'Rosa! Did anything happen?'

'Should I come back?'

'My God,' Stella said, 'is it an emergency? We could
discuss this by mail.'

'You wrote me I should come back.'

'I'm not a millionaire,' Stella said. 'What's the point
of this call?'

'Tree's here.'

'Tree? What's that?'

'*Doctor* Tree. You sent me his letter, he's after me.
By accident I found out where he stays.'

'No one's after you,' Stella said grimly.

Rosa said, 'Maybe I should come back and open up
again.'

'You're talking nonsense. You *can't*. The store's
finished. If you come back it has to be a new attitude
absolutely, recuperated. The end of morbidness.'

'A very fancy hotel,' Rosa said. 'They spend like
kings.'

'It's none of your business.'

'A Tree is none of my business? He gets rich on our

blood! Prestige! People respect him! A professor with specimens! He wrote me baboons!'

'You're supposed to be recuperating,' Stella said; she was wide awake. 'Walk round. Keep out of trouble. Put on your bathing suit. Mingle. How's the weather?'

'In that case you come here,' Rosa said.

'Oh my God, I can't afford it. You talk like I'm a millionaire. What would I do down there?'

'I don't like it alone. A man stole my underwear.'

'Your *what*?' Stella squealed.

'My panties. There's plenty perverts in the streets. Yesterday in the sand I saw two naked men.'

'Rosa,' Stella said, 'if you want to come back, come back. I wrote you that, that's all I said. But you could get interested in something down there for a change. If not a job, a club. If it doesn't cost too much, I wouldn't mind paying for a club. You could join some kind of group, you could walk, you could swim – '

'I already walked.'

'Make friends.' Stella's voice tightened. 'Rosa, this is long *dis*tance.'

On that very phrase, 'long *dis*tance,' Magda sprang to life. Rosa took the shawl and put it over the knob of the receiver: it was like a little doll's head then. She kissed it, right over Stella's admonitions. 'Good-bye,' she told Stella, and didn't care what it had cost. The whole room was full of Magda: she was like a butterfly, in this corner and in that corner, all at once. Rosa waited to see what age Magda was going to be: how nice, a girl of sixteen; girls in their bloom move so swiftly that their blouses and skirts balloon; they are always butterflies at sixteen. There was Magda, all in flower. She was wearing one of Rosa's dresses from high school. Rosa was glad: it was the sky-colored dress, a middling blue with black buttons seemingly made of round chips of coal, like the unlit shards of stars. Persky could never have been acquainted with buttons like that, they were so black and so sparkling; original, with irregular facets like bits of true coal from a vein in the earth or some other planet. Magda's hair was still as yellow as buttercups, and so slippery and fine that her two barrettes, in the shape of cornets, kept sliding down toward the sides of her chin – that chin which was the marvel of her face; with a different kind of chin it would have been a much less explicit face. The jaw was ever so slightly too long, a deepened oval, so that her mouth, especially the lower lip, was not crowded but rather made a definite mark in the middle of spaciousness. Consequently the mouth seemed as significant as a body arrested in orbit, and Magda's sky-filled eyes, nearly rectangular at the corners, were like two obeisant satellites. Magda could be seen with great clarity. She had begun to resemble Rosa's father, who had also a long oval face anchored by a positive mouth. Rosa was enraptured by Magda's healthy forearms. She would have given everything to set her before an easel, to see whether she could paint in watercolors; or to have her seize a violin, or a chess queen; she knew little about Magda's mind at this age, or whether she had any talents; even what her intelligence tended toward. And also she was always a little suspicious of Magda, because of the other strain, whatever it was, that ran in her. Rosa herself was not truly suspicious, but Stella was, and that induced perplexity in Rosa. The other strain was ghostly, even dangerous. It was as if the peril hummed out from the filaments of Magda's hair, those narrow bright wires.

My Gold, my Wealth, my Treasure, my Hidden
Sesame, my Paradise, my Yellow Flower, my Magda!
Queen of Bloom and Blossom!

When I had my store I used to 'meet the public', and I wanted to tell everybody – not only our story, but other stories as well. Nobody knew anything. This amazed me, that nobody remembered what happened only a little while ago. They didn't remember because they didn't know. I'm referring to certain definite facts. The tramcar in the Ghetto, for instance. You know they took the worst section, a terrible slum, and they built a wall around it. It was a regular city neighborhood, with rotting old tenements. They pushed in half a million people, more than double the number there used to be in that place. Three families, including all their children and old folks, into one apartment. Can you imagine a family like us – my father who had been the director-general of the Bank of Warsaw, my sheltered mother, almost Japanese in her shyness and refinement, my two young brothers, my older brother, and me – all of us, who had lived in a tall house with four floors and a glorious attic (you could touch the top of the house by sticking your arm far out its window; it was like pulling the whole green ribbon of summer indoors) – imagine confining *us* with teeming Mockowiczes and Rabinowiczes and Perskys and Finkelsteins, with all their bad-smelling grandfathers and their hordes of feeble children! The children were half dead, always sitting on boxes in tatters with such sick eyes, pus on the lids and the pupils too wildly lit up. All these families used up their energies with walking up and down, and bowing, and shaking and quaking over old rags of prayer books, and their children sat on the boxes and yelled prayers too. We thought they didn't know how to organize themselves in adversity, and besides that, we were furious: because the same sort of adversity was happening to *us* – my father was a person of real importance, and my tall mother had so much delicacy and dignity that people would bow automatically, even before they knew who she was. So we were furious in every direction, but most immediately we were furious because we had to be billeted with such a class, with these old Jew peasants worn out from their rituals and superstitions, phylacteries on their foreheads sticking up so stupidly, like unicorn horns, every morning. And in the most repulsive slum, deep in slops and vermin and a toilet not fit for the lowest criminal. We were not of a background to show our fury, of course, but my father told my brothers and me that my mother would not be able to live through it, and he was right.

In my store I didn't tell this to everyone; who would have the patience to hear it all out? So I used to pick out one little thing here, one little thing there, for each customer. And if I saw they were in a hurry – most of them were, after I began –

I would tell just about the tramcar. When I told about the tramcar, no one ever understood it ran on tracks! Everybody always thought of buses. Well, they couldn't tear up the tracks, they couldn't get rid of the overhead electric wire, could they? The point is they couldn't reroute the whole tram system; so, you know, they didn't. The tramcar came right through the middle of the Ghetto. What they did was build a sort of overhanging pedestrian bridge for the Jews, so they couldn't get near the tramcar to escape on it into the other part of Warsaw. The other side of the wall.

The most astounding thing was that the most ordinary streetcar, bumping along on the most ordinary trolley tracks, and carrying the most ordinary citizens going from one section of Warsaw to another, ran straight into the place of our misery. Every day, and several times a day, we had these witnesses. Every day they saw us – women with shopping sacks; and once I noticed a head of lettuce sticking up out of the top of a sack – green lettuce! I thought my salivary glands would split with aching for that leafy greenness. And girls wearing hats. They were all the sort of plain people of the working class with slovenly speech who ride tramcars, but they were considered better than we, because no one regarded us as Poles anymore. And we, my father, my mother – we had so many pretty jugs on the piano and shining little tables, replicas of Greek vases, and one an actual archaeological find that my father had dug up on a school vacation in his teens, on a trip to Crete – it was all pieced together, and the missing parts, which broke up the design of a warrior with a javelin, filled in with reddish clay. And on the walls, up and down the corridors and along the stairs, we had wonderful ink drawings, the black so black and miraculous, how it measured out a hand and then the shadow of the hand. And with all this – especially our Polish, the way my parents enunciated Polish in soft calm voices with the most precise articulation, so that every syllable struck its target – the people in the tramcar were regarded as Poles – well, they *were*, I don't take it away from them, though they took it away from us – and we were not! They, who couldn't read one line of Tuwim, never mind Virgil, and my father, who knew nearly the whole first half of the *Aeneid* by heart. And in this place now I am like the woman who held the lettuce in the tramcar. I said all this in my store, talking to the deaf. How I became like the woman with the lettuce.

Rosa wanted to explain to Magda still more about the jugs and the drawings on the walls, and the old things in the store, things that nobody cared about, broken chairs with carved birds, long strings of glass beads, gloves and wormy muffs abandoned in drawers. But she was tired from writing so much, even though this time she was not using her regular pen, she was writing inside a blazing flying current, a terrible beak of light bleeding out a kind of cuneiform on the underside of her brain. The drudgery of reminiscence brought fatigue, she felt glazed, lethargic. And Magda! Already she was turning away. Away. The blue of her dress was now only a speck in Rosa's eye. Magda did not even stay to claim her letter: there it flickered, unfinished like an ember, and all because of the ringing from the floor near the bed. Voices, sounds, echoes, noise – Magda collapsed at any stir, fearful as a phantom. She behaved at these moments as if she was ashamed, and hid herself. Magda, my beloved, don't be ashamed! Butterfly, I am not ashamed of your presence: only come to me, come to me again, if no longer now, then later, always come. These were Rosa's private words; but she was stoic, tamed; she did not say them aloud to Magda. Pure Magda, head as bright as a lantern.

The shawled telephone, little grimy silent god, so long comatose – now, like Magda, animated at will, ardent with its cry. Rosa let it clamor once or twice and then heard the Cuban girl announce – oh, 'announce'! – Mr Persky: should he come up or would she come down? A parody of a real hotel! – of, in fact, the MARIE LOUISE, with its fountains, its golden thrones, its thorned wire, its burning Tree!

'He's used to crazy women, so let him come up,' Rosa told the Cuban. She took the shawl off the phone.

Magda was not there. Shy, she ran from Persky. Magda was away.